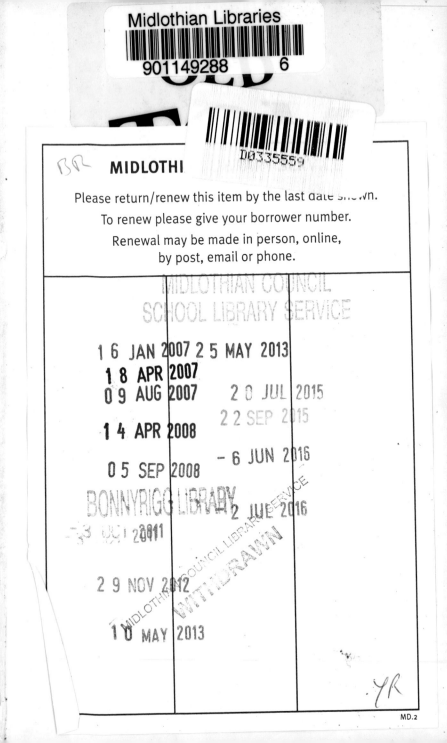

For Peter Marks, Vince Appleby
& Julia Murray

Published by
Happy Cat Books
An imprint of Catnip Publishing Ltd
Islington Business Centre
3-5 Islington High Street
London N1 9LQ

First published by Penguin Books, Australia, 1997

This edition first published 2006
1 3 5 7 9 10 8 6 4 2

Text copyright © Leigh Hobbs, 1997
Illustrations copyright © Leigh Hobbs, 1997
The moral rights of the author/illustrator have been asserted

ISBN 10: 1 905117 13 2
ISBN 13: 978-1-905117-13-0

Printed in Poland

www.catnippublishing.co.uk

OLD
TOM
Goes to Mars

Written and Illustrated by

Leigh HOBBS

HAPPY CAT BOOKS

One day, Angela Throgmorton
saw a sweet little house for sale.
'I must have it for my big baby,' she said.

'Do you deliver?' she asked.
'Of course, madam,' came the reply.
'Good, then I'll take it.'

Soon afterwards,
Old Tom's little house arrived.

'I've a surprise for you, Old Tom,' said Angela,
interrupting his late-afternoon nap.

'It's called a playhouse.
You can keep all your things in there.'

Old Tom loved surprises,
and this one was very special.

There were buttons and levers
and dials and switches.

So Old Tom pressed,

and pushed,

and turned,

and fiddled.

'This little house could do with a clean,'
said Angela Throgmorton.

So she dusted,

and swept,

sponged, and scrubbed.

She was certainly fussy

when it came to her cleaning.

And it was while she was wiping,

that Angela discovered Old Tom had a secret.

He had found a map, and was going to Mars.

Angela tried to change Old Tom's plans.

She thought a nice story might distract him.
But his mind was made up.

Old Tom was off to outer space.

So Angela decided to help.
She made pretty curtains,

and sewed a special
cushion for his trip.

She even made smart striped awnings
in case Old Tom flew too close to the sun.

'What an improvement,'
said Angela, 'even if I do say so myself.'

Angela baked a cake
for Old Tom's journey,

and his favourite biscuits too.

Helping in the kitchen made Old Tom tired.

So he relaxed a little,
and thought about his trip.

He couldn't wait to meet a Martian,
and make new Martian friends.

And if they made him King of Mars . . .

he could eat and drink . . .

everything
that he wanted.

Just then a Martian spoke,
and Old Tom woke up.

'I wouldn't mind some help
around the house!' it said.

So while Angela
cleaned up *someone's* mess,

Old Tom assembled his essential
Mars survival kit.

Angela had made Old Tom
a splendid space suit.

'You can wear this on Mars.
Try it on now!'

'And here's a lovely helmet
to go with it!'

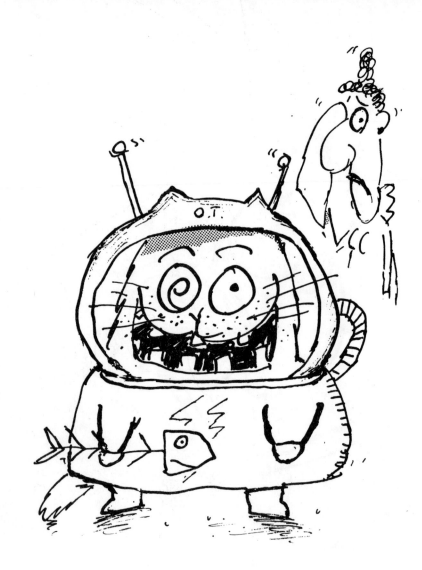

'You look wonderful!' said Angela,
as she wiped away a little tear.

In the evening, Old Tom
did some last-minute packing,

and then got ready for bed.

'You'll need a good night's sleep if you're off to Mars tomorrow,' snapped Angela Throgmorton.

For once,
Old Tom did what he was told.

But Angela tossed and turned all night.

After breakfast, she reminded
Old Tom to be careful,

then farewelled her brave little spaceman.

It was time for him to go.

'Don't forget your lunch!'
said Angela Throgmorton.

She was already missing him terribly,

when suddenly Angela spied a
spot she hadn't scrubbed.

So she scampered up a ladder . . .

as Old Tom prepared for blast off.

At last the time had come!

He turned his dials
and pressed his buttons.

With a bang and a roar
and a flash,
Old Tom left earth,

bound for Mars at last.

Old Tom's essential Mars
survival kit rolled about

as he activated the extra thruster to
escape earth's gravity.

As Old Tom shot
through the sky,

he peered out for one last look,

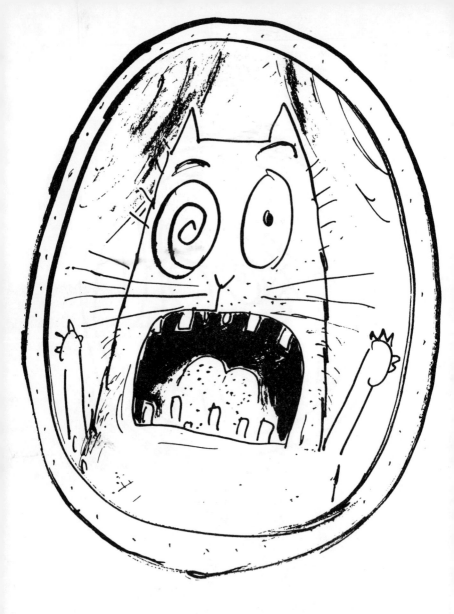

and saw something frightful.

Old Tom was not alone.

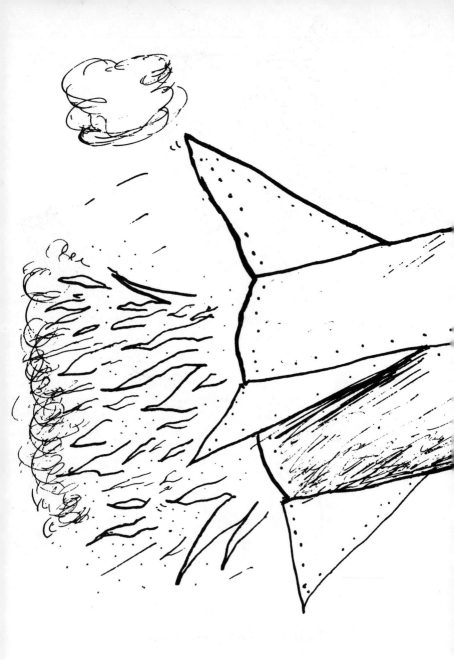

Angela Throgmorton
was Mars-bound too.

The view was spectacular.

But, inside, the danger light was flashing.

Old Tom was off course . . .
and overloaded.

Angela was angry.

She had work to do at home,

and now she was off . . .

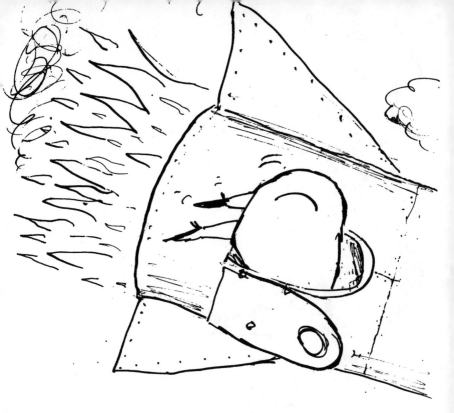

to outer space.

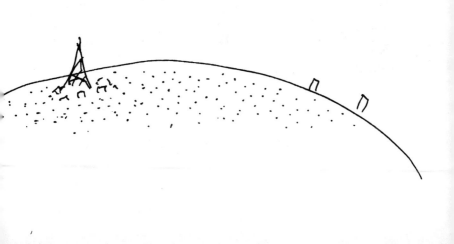

Old Tom wrestled with the controls.

Angela was no help at all.

They hurtled towards Mars

as Angela served afternoon tea.

'We're here!' she shrieked.
Angela was excited too.

Old Tom prepared for landing.
He wanted to make a good impression.

He put on the brakes,

and disengaged the thruster.

His arrival caused a sensation.

Old Tom wanted to make new friends,

but the Martians wouldn't play.

'This doesn't look like Mars to me!'
cried Angela Throgmorton.

It had been a long, long trip . . .

and Angela was a wreck.

Old Tom's adventure was over,

Angela's too.

She was glad to be home.

'There'll be no more trips to Mars
for us,' said Angela Throgmorton.

While she settled back into
life on earth,

Old Tom stayed in his room and sulked.
Only one thing could cheer him up.

And it arrived early the next morning.

Old Tom had promised to be good.

'Let's hope it lasts!'
said Angela Throgmorton.

AUTHOR PHOTOGRAPH BY PETER GREY

About Leigh Hobbs

Leigh Hobbs was born in Melbourne in 1953, but grew up in a country town called Bairnsdale.

Leigh wrote and illustrated *Horrible Harriet*, which was shortlisted for the 2002 Children's Book Council of Australia Book of the year Awards (Picture Books). As well as *Old Tom, Old Tom Goes to the Beach, Old Tom Goes to Mars, and Old Tom's Guide to Being Good* (Happy Cat Books), Leigh wrote and illustrated in full colour *Old Tom's Holiday* for Little Hare. His latest picture book is *Fiona the Pig*.

Leigh is also a sculptor and painter. He has a passion for English history and London is his favourite city, which he visits as often as possible.

Leigh has two dogs, a Blue Heeler and a Kelpie. He feels no affinity with cats, however, he may well admit to one exception ...

www.leighhobbs.com

Read these books and join Old Tom on all his adventures

'Old Tom – a free spirit,
at all times inquisitive,
fearless and ready
for action ... a bold
and economical line
captures every posture and
gesture'

Books for Keeps